Dear Parents:

Congratulations! Your child is taking the first steps on an exciting journey. The destination? Independent reading!

STEP INTO READING® will help your child get there. The program offers five steps to reading success. Each step includes fun stories and colorful art or photographs. In addition to original fiction and books with favorite characters, there are Step into Reading Non-Fiction Readers, Phonics Readers and Boxed Sets, Sticker Readers, and Comic Readers—a complete literacy program with something to interest every child.

Learning to Read, Step by Step!

Ready to Read   Preschool–Kindergarten
• big type and easy words • rhyme and rhythm • picture clues
For children who know the alphabet and are eager to begin reading.

Reading with Help   Preschool–Grade 1
• basic vocabulary • short sentences • simple stories
For children who recognize familiar words and sound out new words with help.

Reading on Your Own   Grades 1–3
• engaging characters • easy-to-follow plots • popular topics
For children who are ready to read on their own.

Reading Paragraphs   Grades 2–3
• challenging vocabulary • short paragraphs • exciting stories
For newly independent readers who read simple sentences with confidence.

Ready for Chapters   Grades 2–4
• chapters • longer paragraphs • full-color art
For children who want to take the plunge into chapter books but still like colorful pictures.

STEP INTO READING® is designed to give every child a successful reading experience. The grade levels are only guides; children will progress through the steps at their own speed, developing confidence in their reading.

Remember, a lifetime love of reading starts with a single step!

Step into Reading, Random House, and the Random House colophon are registered trademarks of Penguin Random House LLC.

Visit us on the Web!
StepIntoReading.com
randomhousekids.com

Educators and librarians, for a variety of teaching tools, visit us at RHTeachersLibrarians.com

ISBN 978-1-5247-2057-5 (trade) — ISBN 978-1-5247-2058-2 (lib.bdg.)

Printed in the United States of America   10 9 8 7 6 5 4 3 2 1

Winter Wishes!

by Kristen L. Depken

based on the teleplay "Shiver and Shake"
by Greg Weisman

illustrated by Dave Aikins

Random House 🏠 New York

One day,
Shimmer and Shine
build a giant snowman.

Their friends

Leah and Layla help.

Their pets help, too!

Zia and Neva
are ice sprites.
They want
to play their own
frosty games.

First, they race
on magic carpets.

Leah and the genies
ride above.
The ice sprites
ride below.

The sprites use magic.

They make

both carpets go faster!

Oh, no!
The pets fall off.

Leah uses a wish.

Everyone arrives safely

at the genies' palace.

Next, Zia and Neva
want to play
frosty hide-and-seek.
They fill the palace
with snow!

Oh, no!

Leah wishes

the snow away.

Then the sprites want
to have a skating race.
They cover the kitchen
with ice.

Leah and the genies
chase Zia and Neva.
They slip on the ice!

Leah wishes
the ice away.

Zia and Neva cannot

finish their skating race.

The sprites
will bowl instead.
They make ice pins
and snowballs.

They roll the balls
and hit the pins.
Leah has no more
wishes to stop them!

The sprites make
a giant snowball.
They get stuck in it
and roll away!

The genies help.

They make an ice ramp.

The snowball rolls

up the ramp.

It flies through the air!

The genies make
a big pile of snow.
The snowball
lands in the snow pile.

The sprites are safe!
They thank the genies.

The new friends
team up and build
a new snowman!